The Dancing Deer
and the
Foolish Hunter

ELISA KLEVEN

Dutton Children's Books New York

*"Whenever we try to isolate anything in the universe,
we find that it's hitched up to everything else."*
—JOHN MUIR

Copyright © 2002 by Elisa Kleven
All rights reserved.

CIP Data is available.

Published in the United States 2002 by Dutton Children's Books,
a division of Penguin Putnam Books for Young Readers
345 Hudson Street, New York, New York 10014
www.penguinputnam.com

Designed by Alyssa Morris
Printed in Hong Kong
First Edition
ISBN 0-525-46832-3
1 3 5 7 9 10 8 6 4 2

For Thacher and Olivia Hurd

Deep in a green forest down by the sea, a hunter spied a little deer dancing.

She danced so joyfully that the birds and the trees around her danced, too. Even the sea seemed to dance.

"Would you look at that!" the hunter said, setting down his gun. "Wowie-kazowie, a dancing deer! A deer I can sell to the circus! Great gumballs—my fortune is made!"

With a lightning-swift swirl of his lasso, the hunter caught the deer . . .

. . . and led her to his house on the edge of town.

Once at home, the hunter waited for the deer to dance again. But she just crouched miserably in the corner.

"Okay, now dance!" the hunter scolded. "Dance like you danced in the forest!"

"To dance I need music," the deer said.

"Great gizzards!" the hunter exclaimed. "Not just a dancing deer— a talking deer, too! Well, here's some music for you."

The hunter turned on his radio. A screechy voice blared out, "Crispy-wispy chips galore! Buy some now! You'll want some more!"

The deer covered her ears. "How can I dance to that noise?" she asked. "To dance, I need the sweet singing of birds."

"Birds?" said the hunter. "To dance you need *birds*? Oh, gee whiz. I guess I'll have to go back to the forest again."

Determined to make the deer dance, he stomped back to the forest, snared two songbirds, *swash-swish* . . .

. . . took them back to his house, and locked them in a cage.

"Sing!" the hunter shouted. "Sing so the deer will dance!"

The birds hid their heads in their wings.

"They're too shy to sing by themselves," said the deer. "To sing, they need the pine trees whistling along with them."

"Trees, peas," scoffed the hunter. "I'll whistle for them myself!"

He whistled loud and shrill, and the birds shrank back in fear.

"They need the pine trees!" said the deer. "The softly whistling, sweet-smelling pines."

"Okay, okay," the hunter grumbled. "I'll get some pine trees, then."

Determined to make the birds sing, the hunter tramped back to the forest, uprooted two small pine trees, *aargh!* . . .

. . . lugged them back to his house, and propped them in a corner.

"Whistle, you dumb trees!" the hunter commanded. "Whistle so the birds will sing!"

But the pine trees simply drooped.

"How can they whistle without the sea breeze blowing softly through them?" the deer asked.

The hunter scratched his head. "How about if I turn on the air conditioner?"

"It wouldn't be the same," said the deer. "To whistle, the pine trees need the sea breeze, soft and wild and fresh."

"Okay, okay," the hunter griped. "I'll get some sea breeze, then."

Determined to make the pine trees whistle, he tromped back to the forest, bottled some sea breeze, *zwip-zwap* . . .

. . . and took it back to his house.

"Blow, breeze!" yelled the hunter. "Blow so the pine trees will whistle!"

But the sea breeze wouldn't blow.

"How can it blow without the salty sea to move it?" asked the deer.

"I'll pour some salt into a glass of water," the hunter offered.

"No, no!" said the deer. "To blow, the sea breeze needs the sea—the sun-spangled, cloud-dappled, deep, fish-filled sea . . . the moving, inspiring sea!"

"Inspiring, perspiring," muttered the hunter. "Okay, okay, I'll get some sea."

Determined to make the sea breeze blow, he marched down to the seashore, filled a bowl with seawater, *gloosh* . . .

. . . and carried it back to his house.

"Move!" he ordered the seawater. "Move so the sea breeze will blow!"

But of course the seawater didn't budge.

"How can it move without the fish, filling it with life?" asked the deer.

"Life, shmife!" retorted the hunter. He rummaged through his freezer, pulled out a box of fish sticks, and plopped one into the bowl of seawater. "Here's some fish," he told the seawater. "Happy?"

"Of course it's not happy!" said the deer. "The seawater needs the splashing, flashing, leaping, *living* fish to be happy!"

"Okay, okay," the hunter said. "I think I get the picture."

Determined to make the seawater move, he ran back to the sea, netted a small fish, *wiggle-squiggle* . . .

. . . rushed it back to his house, and tossed it into the bowl of seawater—where the small fish sank like a stone.

"What's wrong now?" the hunter asked.

"He probably misses his mother," the deer said.

"His mother!" snapped the hunter. "How am I supposed to find his mother? The sea is a pretty big place, you know!"

"Who says you have to find his mother?" said the deer. "Just put the fish back in the sea, and he'll find her all by himself."

"But if I put the fish back in the sea, then the bowl of seawater won't have anything to fill it with life!" cried the hunter.

"Pour the seawater back into the sea, too," suggested the deer. "Then it will fill with life all by itself."

"But if I pour back the seawater, then what will make the sea breeze blow?" the hunter asked.

"Put the sea breeze back into the fresh air," urged the deer. "Then it will blow by itself."

"But if I put back the sea breeze, then what will make the pine trees whistle?"

"The pine trees will whistle by themselves," said the deer, "if you plant them in the breezy forest again."

"But if I plant the pine trees in the forest, then the birds won't sing!" argued the hunter.

"Don't worry about the birds," said the deer. "They'll sing just fine, once you put them back in the forest, too."

"No," said the hunter. "That will never do. For if I put back the birds, then who will make music for you? You didn't like the radio. If I put back the birds, I'll *never* get you to dance!"

"Hunter! Stop your foolishness!" the deer cried. "Just put me back in the deep green forest, along with everything else, and I'll dance all by myself!"

"But if I put you back, you'll run away," said the hunter. "And I won't be able to sell you to the circus. I'd get a lot of money for a dancing deer, you know!"

"Listen," said the deer, "I have an idea. Why don't you just dress up in a deer costume and dance at the circus yourself? You would probably make a lot of money *that* way!"

"But I don't know how to dance," said the hunter.

"Return me to the forest, and I'll show you," replied the deer.

"You promise?" asked the hunter.

"I promise," said the deer.

So, eager to learn to dance, the hunter
went back to the forest. And then, with a
swash and a *swish*,

a *pat-patting* of earth,

a *whish* and a *whoosh*,

a *gloosh* and a *sloosh,*

a *wiggle* and a *squiggle* and a happy *splash,* he put back everything he had snared and caged and uprooted and bottled and netted and lassoed. And everything sang and whistled and blew and moved . . .

and danced as it had before!

"Now you try," the deer told the hunter.

The hunter took a few clumsy steps. "Good try!" encouraged the deer. "A nice start."

"Really?" asked the hunter, dancing some more. "You think I'm a good dancer?"

"A very good dancer," replied the deer, taking a few steps away from him. "The spirit's there!"

"Great gooseberries!" laughed the hunter. No one had ever given him such praise. He twirled and bowed.

"Wonderful!" cheered the deer, dancing deeper into the forest. "Isn't it fun?"

"Even more fun than hunting!" yelled the hunter, leaping and jumping.

"Much more fun than hunting," called the deer as she danced out of sight. "Keep dancing, now!"

"I will!" said the hunter. "You, too!"
The hunter swirled and spun through the night. He danced so
joyfully that the birds and the trees around him danced, too. Even
the sea seemed to dance.

And, though he never joined the circus, the hunter (or should we call him the dancer?) is dancing still.

Now and again, the deer comes out to see him.